W9-DFQ-834

VESTAVIA HILLS
PUBLIC LIBRARY

1112 Montgomery Highway
Vestavia Hills, Alabama 35216

Winter Blanket

Written by Larry Dane Brimner • Illustrated by R. W. Alley

E
BrimL

Published in the United States of America by The Child's World®
PO Box 326 • Chanhassen, MN 55317-0326
800-599-READ • www.childsworld.com

Reading Adviser

Cecilia Minden-Cupp, PhD, Director of Language and Literacy, Harvard University Graduate School of Education, Cambridge, Massachusetts

Acknowledgments

The Child's World®: Mary Berendes, Publishing Director

Editorial Directions, Inc.: E. Russell Primm, Editorial Director and Project Manager; Katie Marsico, Associate Editor; Judith Shiffer, Assistant Editor; Matt Messbarger, Editorial Assistant

The Design Lab: Kathleen Petelinsek, Design and Art Production

Copyright © 2006 by The Child's World®
All rights reserved. No part of this book may be reproduced or utilized in any form or by any means without written permission from the publisher.

Library of Congress Cataloging-in-Publication Data

Brimner, Larry Dane.
  Winter blanket / written by Larry Dane Brimner ; illustrated by R. W. Alley.
    p. cm. — (Magic door to learning)
  Summary: A child describes some of the sights and sounds of winter.
  ISBN 1-59296-520-2 (lib. bdg. : alk. paper) [1. Winter—Fiction.] I. Alley, R. W. (Robert W.), ill. II. Title.
  PZ7.B767Wi 2005
  [E]—dc22   2005005365

A book is a door, a magic door.
It can take you places
you have never been before.
Ready? Set?
Turn the page.
Open the door.
Now it is time to explore.

Winter is a soft, white blanket
that wraps everything in quiet.

Swish. Swoosh.
It is the gentle sound
of skates on ice.

Crunch. Scritch.

It is the noise made by Dad's
boots on newly fallen snow.

Yawning,
I stretch and get up.
The logs in the
fireplace crackle and
snap like popcorn.

I wiggle my toes by the fire and look
out the window while I have breakfast.

Outside, penguins
glide across the pond.

13

Later, Mom bundles
me in shirts and jackets,
and I grow rounder
and rounder until I
am a balloon hardly
able to move at all.

15

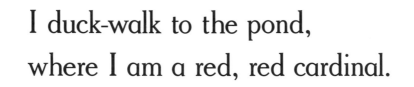

I duck-walk to the pond,
where I am a red, red cardinal.

16

Round and round we go,
the penguins and I.

Our laughter is lost
in the blankets of snow,
lost among the leafless
trees around the pond.

Then Mom calls me inside
for some hot, hot chocolate.

And while winter wraps
everything in quiet,
Mom wraps me in
a blanket of warmth.

Our story is over, but there is still much to explore beyond the magic door!

Did you know that every snowflake is different? With an adult's help, use scissors to cut out paper snowflakes. Create a variety of designs and patterns so that your snowflakes are as unique as those that fall from the sky!

These books will help you explore at the library and at home:

Plourde, Lynn, and Greg Couch. *Winter Waits*. New York: Simon & Schuster Books for Young Readers, 2001.

Scott, Evelyn, and Virginia Parsons (illustrator). *The Fourteen Bears in Summer and Winter*. New York: Random House Children's Books, 2005.

About the Author

Larry Dane Brimner is an award-winning author of more than 120 books for children. When he isn't at his computer writing, he can be found biking in Colorado or hiking in Arizona. You can visit him online at *www.brimner.com*.

About the Illustrator

R. W. Alley has illustrated more than seventy-five books for children and has authored five of these. Since 1997, he has served as the illustrator on Michael Bond's Paddington Bear series. Alley lives in Barrington, Rhode Island, with his wife and two children. He often visits local elementary schools to discuss how words and pictures come together to form books.

VESTAVIA HILLS
LIBRARY IN THE FOREST
1221 MONTGOMERY HWY.
VESTAVIA HILLS, AL 35216
205-978-0155